SCARY
SCOTT

'Scary Scott'
An original concept by Katie Dale
© Katie Dale

Illustrated by Irene Montano

Published by MAVERICK ARTS PUBLISHING LTD

Studio 3A, City Business Centre, 6 Brighton Road,

Horsham, West Sussex, RH13 5BB

© Maverick Arts Publishing Limited January 2019

+44 (0)1403 256941

A CIP catalogue record for this book is available at the British Library.

ISBN 978-1-84886-398-9

www.maverickbooks.co.uk

Gold

This book is rated as: Gold Band (Guided Reading)

SCARY SCOTT

By **Katie Dale**

Illustrated by **Irene Montano**

Chapter 1

There were a lot of good things about being a ghost. Scott could fly, which was *great* fun. "Whee!" he cried, as he looped-the-loop around all the chimneys in town.

Scott could also move through walls. This meant he never had to pay to go to the cinema. He got to see all the latest movies for free (which was lucky, as he didn't have any money).

It also meant he never got locked out of his house (which was lucky as he didn't have a key).

In fact, Scott didn't even have to buy his house. He just chose a nice big empty one that was for sale and moved in. He was going to leave when someone bought the house. But for some reason, no-one ever had.

5

Scott didn't have any parents, so he could go wherever he wanted and stay up as late as he liked (which was lucky, as Scott never slept).

Yes, there were lots of good things about being a ghost.

But there was also one BIG BAD thing...

Everyone was scared of Scott.

Whenever he entered a room, everyone ran away screaming. That wasn't much fun. It was actually pretty horrible. And very lonely.

Scott hated scaring people so much that he ended up only going out at night, when everyone else was fast asleep.

But even then he sometimes accidentally scared people.

More than anything, Scott wanted a friend.

Then one night Scott saw a poster for a party. A Halloween party!

There were pictures of ghosts and vampires and witches all over it.

It must be a party for ghosts, vampires and witches! I can finally make some friends! Hurray!

Chapter 2

Scott couldn't wait for the party. He counted down the days. It was all he could think about. Then finally it was Halloween night.

As Scott approached the house it was filled

with lights and music and laughter. He knocked nervously on the door and a witch opened it!

"Welcome!" she cried. "Come in and join the party!"

"Thanks!" Scott said, grinning.

The house was full of monsters and vampires and mummies. It was amazing!

They played bobbing for doughnuts...

Wrap-the-mummy...

Pin-the-stalk-on-the-pumpkin...

Then they raced spiders, carved pumpkins and told ghost stories! Scott had never had such a great time!

There was time for one last game.

"Let's play Guess Who," a witch next to Scott said.

"Yes!" everyone cried, but Scott frowned. He didn't know that game.

"I guess that the monster is Ben!" cried the witch.

The monster laughed. Then, to Scott's horror, he pulled his head off! Scott gasped. The monster was just a boy wearing a costume!

"Correct!" the monster-boy said. "My turn. I guess that the witch is Lucy."

Scott stared as the witch pulled off her nose to reveal a smiling little girl.

"Correct!" she laughed.

Scott gulped. Was everyone else a child wearing a scary costume?

His heart beat fast as everyone guessed each other's names. Finally there was only Scott left.

"I guess that the ghost is Dev," Lucy said.

Scott froze. What should he do?

trick
or treat

15

Chapter 3

"Well?" Lucy said. "Am I right? Are you the ghost, Dev?"

Scott didn't reply. He didn't know what to say. So he nodded.

"I knew it!" Lucy said, grinning.

"Time to go trick-or-treating!" Ben cried.

Scott sighed with relief. His secret was safe!

Scott had never been trick-or-treating before. It was great fun!

"Trick-or-treat!" the kids cried as they knocked at every house on the street.

Each neighbour they visited laughed and gave them sweets.

By the time they reached the end of the road, their bag was full! But then a vampire raced towards them.

"Sorry I'm late!" he called.

"Who are you?" Lucy asked.

The vampire laughed and pulled off his mask. "I'm Dev!"

Oh no! Scott froze as everyone turned to stare at him.

"If you're Dev," Ben said, "then who is wearing the ghost costume?"

Scott panicked.

Everyone was about to learn the truth about him. They'd never want to see him again! Worse still, they'd get the fright of their lives!

There was only one thing Scott could do.

Chapter 4

Scott turned to flee, but a group of big boys came round the corner.

"Not so fast," one boy said, blocking Scott's way.

"Oh no!" cried Lucy. "It's Billy and the bullies!"

"Hey trick-or-treaters!" Billy called.

"Give us your sweets!"

Scott frowned. Why should the kids give Billy their sweets?

"W-we'd b-better d-do as he s-says," Ben stammered. "They're much b-bigger than us."

Lucy swallowed hard and stepped forward, holding out the bag of sweets to the bullies.

"Thank you very much!" Billy said, grinning.

"Not so fast!" Scott cried, blocking Billy's way. "Get your own trick-or-treat sweets."

Billy frowned. "Who are you, pipsqueak?"

Scott gritted his teeth. "Who do you think I am? I am a ghost!"

Billy and the bullies laughed.

"Yeah, right!" Billy scoffed. "It's not even a good costume!"

Scott scowled, and put on his best scary voice. "Go away or I will scare your pants off!"

The bullies laughed harder than ever.

Scott stared at them helplessly. He'd never had any trouble scaring people before! But he couldn't let them get away with bullying his friends. Even if they wouldn't be his friends anymore if they knew he was really a ghost.

Chapter 5

"SCRAM!"

Scott yelled, soaring
into the air. He flew
around the bullies,

through a tree, and hovered in mid-air above them.

"And don't **EVER** bully **ANYONE** ever again or I will find you and haunt you **FOREVER!**"

The bullies stopped laughing. They turned very pale.

Then they ran away, screaming.

"We won't!"

"We promise!"

"I want my mummy!"

Scott smiled. Then he felt worried.

He'd scared the bullies away, but what if he'd scared the other kids too?

He turned around nervously, expecting them to have run away too.

But they were still there. They weren't screaming or running.

Instead, they were smiling.

"Thank you," said Lucy, stepping forwards. "Who are you?"

"M-my name's S-Scott," Scott said nervously. "I'm a g-ghost."

"We can see that," said Ben, grinning. "Cool."

"Cool?" Scott said hesitantly. "You mean, you're not scared of me?"

"Of course not!" Lucy laughed. "You just saved us from the bullies! And we've been having fun with you all evening! You're our friend!"

"Hurray for Scott!" Ben cried.

Everybody cheered and Scott's heart soared. He couldn't believe it! He finally had some friends!

The End

Book Bands for Guided Reading

The labels on the left read, from top to bottom: Pink, Red, Yellow, Blue, Green, Orange, Turquoise, Purple, Gold, White.

The Institute of Education book banding system is a scale of colours that reflects the various levels of reading difficulty. The bands are assigned by taking into account the content, the language style, the layout and phonics. Word, phrase and sentence level work is also taken into consideration.

Maverick Early Readers are a bright, attractive range of books covering the pink to white bands. All of these books have been book banded for guided reading to the industry standard and edited by a leading educational consultant.

To view the whole Maverick Readers scheme, visit our website at

www.maverickearlyreaders.com

Or scan the QR code above to view our scheme instantly!